D1278362

WITHDRAWN

Stephen Mackey

Miki

and the Wishing Star

Sandy Creek
NEW YORK

Moonshine, starlight and falling snow,
Watch how the magic begins to grow.
Wishes and dreams — will they ever come true
For Miki and Penguin and Polar Bear, too?

Miki and Penguin and Polar Bear were dreaming through the darkest, deepest winter night, waiting for something wonderful to happen the very next day, because…

...it was their birthday!
"And because it's *everyone's* birthday," said Miki,
"we can *all* have a wish when we blow out the
birthday cake candles."

"Me first! Me first!" squeaked Penguin.
And he closed his eyes and wished a very secret wish.
"I wish I wasn't so very small.
I wish I was the biggest penguin of all!"

And way up in the cold dark sky,
a wishing star burst into a million tiny crystals of magic.

And Penguin got his wish.
"Where is he?" cried Miki anxiously.

"I'm up here!" laughed Penguin.
"And I'm the biggest penguin in the world."

But the biggest penguin in the world was also the hungriest. Polar Bear and Miki cooked him enough fried eggs to fill a wheelbarrow.

"That's only a snack!" complained Penguin, sitting down and nearly squashing Miki's house.

"Then you'll have to find breakfast somewhere else," said Miki.

"I WILL!" said Penguin.
He stomped off, singing:
"I'm the biggest, I'm the best —
I'm much BIGGER than the rest!"

Before long, he met a crowd of scared little penguins marooned on an ice floe.

"Penguin to the rescue!"

he cried, making a bridge.

Then he wrestled with sea monsters!
He really was a big brave penguin.

But Miki and Polar Bear were very worried. Would Penguin ever come home again?

Polar Bear used his birthday wish straight away.

*"I wish our Penguin now to see
exactly as he used to be!"*

And, far, far away the wishing star exploded into countless enchanted splinters of ice.

Penguin began to feel very strange.
He was shrinking,
smaller and smaller and smaller.

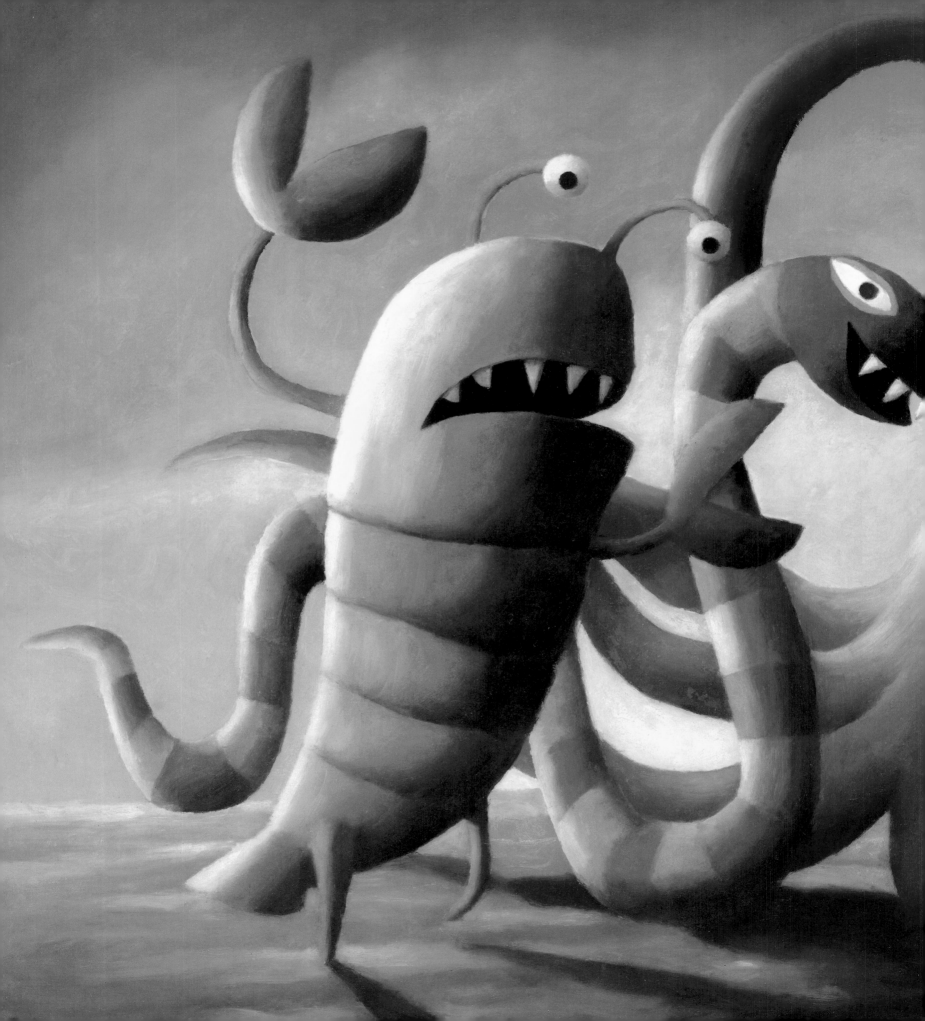

"Oh no!" gulped little Penguin. "I'd better run!"

Things would have turned out very
badly for Penguin if Polar Bear and
Miki hadn't appeared with their ice cannon.

"Over here, Penguin!" cried Miki.
"10-9-8-7-6-5-4-3-2-1 — FIRE!"

The monsters were frozen on the spot.

"Wheeee! Thank you!" squealed all the little penguins. "Now we've got a winter wonderland of our very own. Come back soon and play!"

"That was an exciting birthday,"
said Penguin, when they got home.
"What shall we wish for next year?
Superpowers? I'll be the fastest
penguin in the world. Let's..."

"But first," said Miki, "I'm going to make my birthday wish.

Starlight, moonshine, ice and snow,
I wish that our friendship
will always grow.
Through darkest night,
whatever may be,
We'll stay together,
just us three."

"...go to bed now," yawned Polar Bear.

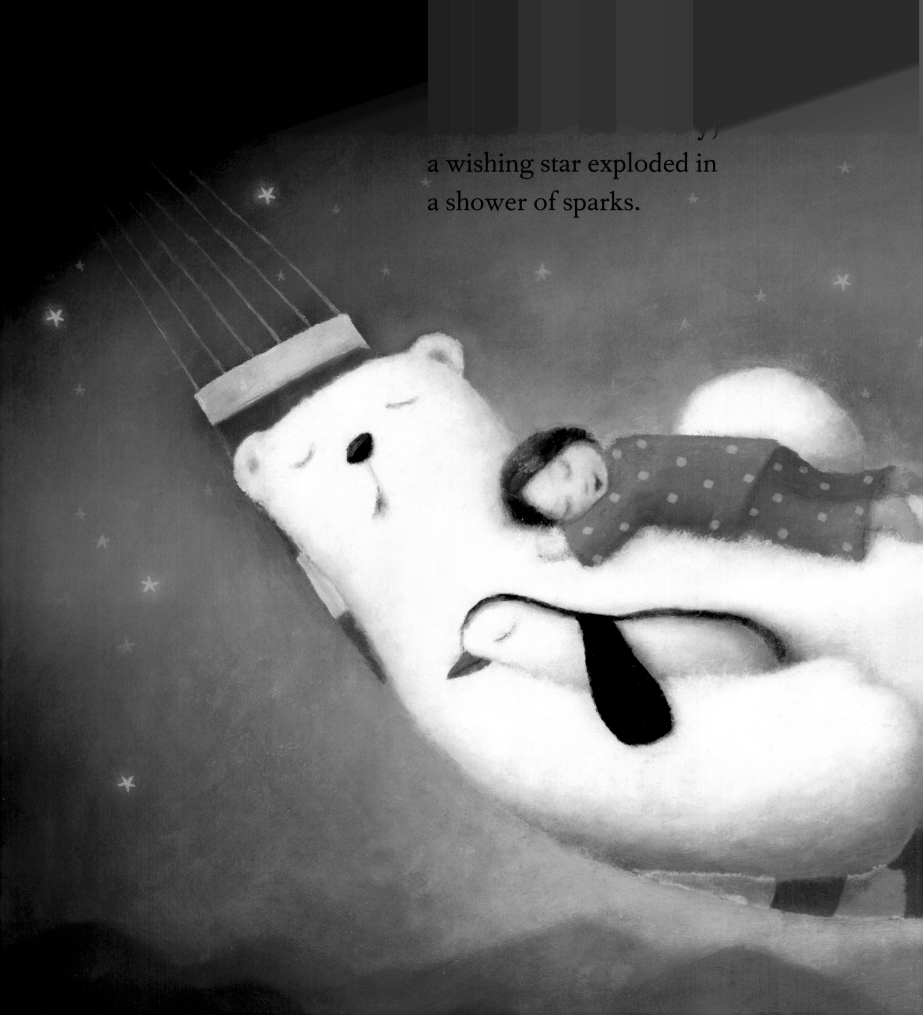

a wishing star exploded in
a shower of sparks.

Miki smiled sleepily. "Night Penguin.
Night Polar Bear."

"Night night Miki," said Polar Bear.
But Penguin was already fast asleep,
racing through the stars in his dreams.

To Mom and Dad

An Imprint of Sterling Publishing
387 Park Avenue South
New York, NY 10016

SANDY CREEK and the distinctive Sandy Creek logo are registered trademarks of Barnes & Noble, Inc.

Text and illustrations © Stephen Mackey 2012

This 2013 edition published by Sandy Creek.

All rights reserved. No part of this publication may be reproduced, stored in a retrieval system or transmitted in any form or by any means (including electronic, mechanical, photocopying, recording, or otherwise) without prior written permission from the publisher.

ISBN 978-1-4351-4998-4

Manufactured in China

Lot #:
2 4 6 8 10 9 7 5 3 1
04/13